Books by Patricia Reilly Giff you will enjoy:

The Lincoln Lions Band books
illustrated by Emily Arnold McCully

MEET THE LINCOLN LIONS BAND
YANKEE DOODLE DRUMSTICKS
THE "JINGLE BELLS" JAM

The Polka Dot Private Eye books
illustrated by Blanche Sims

THE MYSTERY OF THE BLUE RING
THE RIDDLE OF THE RED PURSE
THE SECRET AT THE POLK STREET SCHOOL
THE POWDER PUFF PUZZLE
THE CASE OF THE COOL-ITCH KID
GARBAGE JUICE FOR BREAKFAST
THE TRAIL OF THE SCREAMING TEENAGER
THE CLUE AT THE ZOO

YEARLING BOOKS are designed especially to entertain and enlighten young people. Patricia Reilly Giff, consultant to this series, received her bachelor's degree from Marymount College and a master's degree in history from St. John's University. She holds a Professional Diploma in Reading and a Doctorate of Humane Letters from Hofstra University. She was a teacher and reading consultant for many years, and is the author of numerous books for young readers.

D0058800

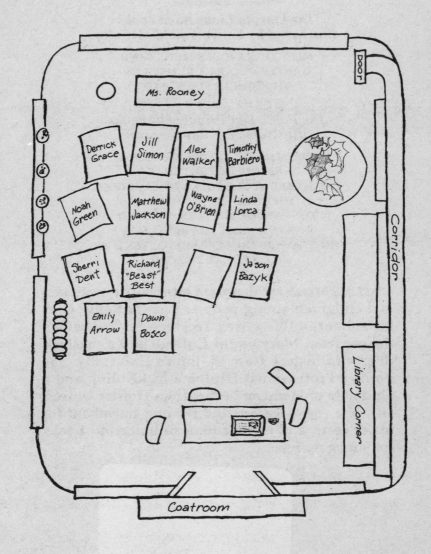

The Kids of the Polk Street School

3

THE CANDY CORN CONTEST

Patricia Reilly Giff

Illustrated by Blanche Sims

A YEARLING BOOK

To *Beverly Horowitz*

Published by
Dell Yearling
an imprint of
Random House Children's Books
a division of Random House, Inc.
1540 Broadway
New York, New York 10036

Visit us on the Web! www.randomhouse.com/kids

Educators and librarians, for a variety of teaching tools, visit us at www.randomhouse.com/teachers

ISBN: 0-440-41072-X

Printed in the United States of America

November 1984

41

OPM

Chapter 1

Ms. Rooney gave out the drawing paper. "All eyes on me," she said.

Richard Best put his hand into his desk.

"This is the way to make a Thanksgiving turkey," said Ms. Rooney. She picked up a fat piece of brown chalk.

Richard fished around for his lunch bag. He watched Ms. Rooney trace her hand on the chalkboard.

He had made a turkey just like that last year . . . and the year before. Now he was making another one.

A left-back turkey. Just like him.

He started to open his lunch bag.

It made a crackling noise.

Matthew Jackson turned around. He pulled on his stick-out ears. "Hi, Beast," he whispered.

Richard made a beast face. He smiled at Matthew.

Matthew was a great kid, Richard thought.

But he wet the bed.

And he probably hadn't taken a bath since last summer.

Sometimes Richard wished Ms. Rooney would change everyone's seat. But then he might end up sitting right in front of her desk.

He pulled a piece of bread off his cheese sandwich and looked at it.

There was a little piece of cheese stuck to the bread.

He scraped the cheese off and flicked it on the floor. Then he sneaked the bread into his mouth.

Ms. Rooney stopped talking. She frowned.

Richard stopped chewing.

Then Ms. Rooney put a round red eye on her turkey.

Richard wished she'd hurry up. He couldn't wait for show-and-tell.

He had some great news.

It was about a sleep-over party the day after Thanksgiving.

3

Beast's friend Emily Arrow put her hand in the air. "You forgot the turkey's feet," she told Ms. Rooney.

"So I did," said Ms. Rooney. She drew two yellow stick legs. She drew a bunch of claws.

Then she wiped her chalky hands on a piece of paper. "I have exciting news," she said.

Richard hoped she didn't know about his party. He wanted to tell everyone himself. He picked up a brown crayon and began to trace his hand for his turkey.

Ms. Rooney went to the closet. She took out a huge jar. She brought it over to her desk.

It was filled with Candy Corn.

Richard felt his mouth water.

"We're going to have a contest," Ms. Rooney said. "Guess how many pieces of Candy Corn are in this jar?"

"Two hundred thousand," Emily Arrow called.

"That's not right," Dawn Bosco said. "Maybe a hundred."

"What's the prize?" Noah Greene asked.

"The whole jar of Candy Corn," Ms. Rooney said. "It will be a Thanksgiving present."

Matthew turned around. He gave Richard a little poke. "I hope I win," he said. "If you win, will you share with me?"

Richard looked down at the picture he had started. It was a good-looking turkey with blue feathers. He made believe he hadn't heard Matthew.

He'd hate to give up half of that Candy Corn if he won.

"How many guesses do we get?" Emily Arrow asked.

"That's the fun part," Ms. Rooney said. "Every time you read a page from your library book, you can take a guess."

Matthew groaned.

"Great," said Timothy Barbiero.

Richard looked at Timothy. Timothy was the fastest reader in the class. He'd probably win.

Too bad.

Emily must have been thinking the same thing, Richard thought. She was looking at Timothy too.

"I'm going to win," she said. "I'm going to try."

"Good for you," said Ms. Rooney.

"I think I'll win," Timothy said. "I can read fast."

Emily looked down at her desk. She didn't say anything.

But Richard knew what she was thinking.

She was a terrible reader.

Just like him.

Richard pulled out his library book.

It was a fat one.

It took him about an hour to get through one page.

He shouldn't have picked such a hard one.

He'd go back to the library this afternoon. He'd pick a nice skinny little book.

"And," said Ms. Rooney, "no cheating. No reading skinny little baby books."

Richard looked at the jar again. He was dying to win.

Matthew was a worse reader than he was.

6

He didn't have a chance of winning, Richard thought.

Poor Matthew.

Poor smelly Matthew.

Richard tapped his arm. "If I win," he said, "I'll share with you."

"All right," Matthew said. Then he shook his head. "We won't win. We're the worst readers in the class."

Chapter 2

It was almost time to go home. Richard was sick of waiting for show-and-tell.

"All right," Ms. Rooney said at last. "Who has something to tell us?"

Richard waved his hand around in the air.

Ms. Rooney picked Emily Arrow.

Emily hurried to the front of the room. She was wearing red sneakers. Her legs looked like Slim Jim pretzels.

"I went to my aunt Helen's wedding on Saturday," Emily said. "I'll tell you all about it."

Richard wiggled around in his seat.

Emily told about the bride's dress and the bridesmaids' dresses.

She told about the wedding cake.

Richard sighed in a loud voice.

Emily danced around in her sneakers. "This is the way the bride danced," she said.

Richard looked at the other kids.

Timothy was reading a book as fast as he could.

He'd have about five guesses by tomorrow.

He might win the jar of Candy Corn before Richard guessed once.

Suddenly Emily saw Timothy reading. She frowned. "I guess that's all," she said. She raced back to her seat and opened her library book.

Ms. Rooney looked around.

Richard put his hand in the air. He knelt up on his seat so Ms. Rooney would look at him.

"Sit down, Richard," Ms. Rooney said. She looked around the room. "Wayne?"

Wayne O'Brien went to the front of the room. He stood there for a minute.

Then he shook his head. "I don't remember what I was going to say."

In front of him Richard could hear Matthew trying to read. He didn't know the words.

At last Wayne raised his shoulders up to his neck. He went back to his seat.

Ms. Rooney smiled at Richard. "Do you have something—"

Richard rushed to the front of the room.

He took a deep breath. "I'm going to have a sleep-over," he said. "Everyone's invited."

Emily looked up from her book. "Great," she said.

Richard swallowed. "I mean, the boys. Only the boys. It's a sleep-over party for boys."

"Oh," said Emily Arrow.

"There isn't room for girls," Richard said.

"All right," Emily said.

"I'm coming," yelled Matthew. "When is it?"

"The night after Thanksgiving," Richard said.

Timothy Barbiero put his hand in the air. "Will there be good stuff to eat?"

"Sure," Richard said. "My mother's making spaghetti and Italian bread. And leftover turkey. And we're going to have ice cream for dessert."

Derrick Grace raised his hand. "I can't come," he said. He looked as if he were going to cry. "I'm going to my uncle John's."

"I can't come either," Jason Bazyk said.

Richard looked around.

Not so good.

Now there would be only six, counting himself.

"Don't worry," Matthew called again. "I'm coming. I love ice cream."

Richard went back to his seat. "You're coming, aren't you?" he called to Timothy Barbiero.

"I think so," Timothy said.

Dawn Bosco was up in the front of the room. "My grandmother lives in Florida," she said.

She held up a fat grapefruit. "My grandmother sent us a whole box of these."

Richard shuddered. He hated grapefruit.

He opened his book to page three. Last week he had read two pages. Maybe he could get two guesses.

As soon as Dawn sat down, he raised his hand. "Can I use last week's book for a guess?"

Ms. Rooney thought for a minute.

"Oh, good," Timothy Barbiero said. "I read about a hundred pages last week."

Ms. Rooney shook her head. "I think we'd better stick to this week. We'll start with today."

Richard looked at page three. He tried to read the first sentence. It was a tough one.

He turned to page four. A nice big picture took up most of the space. He wouldn't have to read many words.

If he ever got there.

Timothy Barbiero raised his hand. "I started my new book this morning," he said. "And now I'm almost finished."

"That's wonderful," Ms. Rooney said.

Richard looked at Timothy. Timothy was smart. And he was lucky.

Richard wished he was like Timothy. He was sick of being dumb. And unlucky.

Chapter 3

"Can anyone tell us about the first Thanksgiving?" Ms. Rooney asked.

"I can," Timothy Barbiero said.

"Me too," Dawn Bosco said.

Richard hid behind Matthew. He didn't know one thing about the first Thanksgiving.

Six boys would be at his sleep-over. He wrote a big six on the paper. Underneath he wrote a *T* for Timothy. Then he wrote a *W* for Wayne.

"Many years ago," said Ms. Rooney, "some people sailed across the ocean."

Emily Arrow raised her hand. "They came on a boat called the *Mayflower*."

"Right, Emily," said Ms. Rooney. "And the people were called Pilgrims."

Richard wrote an *X* on the paper. *X* for Alex.

He looked around. Who else was coming?

"It was cold," said Ms. Rooney. "The Pilgrims had very little food. Many of them were sick."

Matthew. He had forgotten Matthew.

He wrote an *M* on the paper.

Then he wrote *Beast* for himself. His nickname.

"Timothy," he whispered. "Wayne. Alex. Matthew. And me."

He counted. "One. Two. Three. Four. Five." Someone was missing.

"The Pilgrims' first winter was terrible," Ms. Rooney said.

Noah raised his hand. "Then the Indians came to help them."

"Very good, Noah," Ms. Rooney said.

Richard wrote an *N* for Noah. That was six.

He looked around again. He'd sit next to Timothy when they ate.

Alex would sit on his other side.

He'd put a big pile of spaghetti on his plate.

He'd save some room for ice cream.

"Are you listening, Richard?" Ms. Rooney asked.

Richard jumped. "Yes."

"In the spring," said Ms. Rooney, "the Indians showed the Pilgrims how to plant corn. They told them to put dead fish in the earth with the seed. It would make the corn grow better."

"Yucks," said Emily Arrow.

"Don't be silly, Emily," said Ms. Rooney. "The Indians were right. The corn grew strong."

Richard thought about his sleep-over again.

Everyone would sleep in the den.

He'd sleep next to Timothy and Alex.

Matthew would have to sleep next to the wall. Just in case.

And Wayne would sleep on Matthew's other side.

"The Pilgrims learned to hunt," said Ms. Rooney. "Then they had more food."

Richard wished he had something to eat. Some of that spaghetti. Some leftover turkey.

"Yes," said Ms. Rooney. "The Pilgrims worked hard. Very hard. They did the right thing."

"Then they had a Thanksgiving party," said Timothy.

"Yes," said Ms. Rooney. "They invited everyone."

"Hey," Wayne whispered. "I have to talk to you."

"What's the matter?" Richard asked.

"I'll tell you later," Wayne said. He was frowning.

Richard felt a worried feeling. He hoped Wayne was coming to his party.

It would be nice for Matthew to have someone to sleep near.

Besides, if Wayne didn't come, there would be only five boys.

Chapter 4

But there was no time to talk to Wayne.

They had to pack their books. And Richard had to find his sister, Holly.

For a while Richard waited in the hall.

He looked at the picture of the man on the wall.

JAMES K. POLK, it said underneath.

Poor James K. Polk, Richard thought. His collar was so big, it was flapping around his cheeks.

Richard went to the boys' room.

Holly still didn't come.

He went back to his classroom. Ms. Rooney was gone.

Jim, the custodian, was beginning to sweep.

Richard saw that Matthew had forgotten his sweater. It was on the floor.

He picked it up. It smelled like Matthew.

He put it on Matthew's chair.

"Thanks," Jim said. He finished sweeping. He pushed the broom out to the hall.

Richard walked over to Ms. Rooney's desk.

He looked at the jar of Candy Corn.

His mouth was watering again.

He tried to guess how many pieces of Candy Corn there were.

Maybe he should do some counting.

He could count all the Candy Corn on one side of the jar today.

Tomorrow after school he'd count the ones on the other side.

It wouldn't be cheating, Richard thought. He'd still have to guess how many were in the middle.

He started to count.

After he was half finished, he forgot what number he was up to.

He took off the top of the jar so he could see inside. There were three fat ones on the top.

He'd love to eat the whole jar of Candy Corn right now.

He'd take them two at a time. He'd stick them together. Then he'd crunch right down on them.

He hoped his mother would have lots of Candy Corn for his Thanksgiving sleep-over.

She wouldn't though. She didn't like him to eat too much candy.

He wondered if Ms. Rooney had counted all the Candy Corn yet.

Maybe not.

They'd probably count them together. The whole class. At the end of the guessing.

He poked his finger into the jar.

The Candy Corn clicked together.

It would be easy to dump everything out of the jar. It would be easy to count them.

He'd never do that.

That would really be cheating.

Someone else might do it though.

Ms. Rooney should have locked the jar up in the closet.

He took four pieces of Candy Corn out of the

22

jar. He put them on the desk. He made them into a Candy Corn fence.

They looked neat, like a bunch of pumpkin teeth waiting for a pumpkin.

He picked them up and put them back into the jar. All except one. A fat one.

Without thinking, he popped it into his mouth.

He ate it so fast, he hardly tasted it.

He reached into the jar. He took out another one. Quickly he put it into his mouth.

Then he took a third.

After he had swallowed them, he ran his tongue around his teeth.

His mouth tasted all sugary.

He stared at the jar.

He could feel his heart begin to pound.

He put the top back on the jar.

There was a sound at the door.

"Forgot my sweater," Matthew said.

Richard nodded. He kept his mouth closed tight.

"I wish we'd win," Matthew said.

"Mmm," Richard said. He pressed his lips

together a little harder. He hoped Matthew couldn't smell the Candy Corn.

Maybe Matthew couldn't smell anything, Richard thought. If he could, he might take a bath.

"I saw Ms. Rooney counting all the Candy Corn," Matthew said. "At lunchtime."

"Oh," Richard said.

"She wrote the number right on the bottom of the jar," Matthew said.

"I wouldn't look," Richard said. He tried not to move his lips too much.

"I wouldn't look either," said Matthew. He moved the jar around a little. "Ms. Rooney said we're going to count them again. After someone wins. She said it will be a good math lesson."

"Oh," Richard said again.

"I'm going to work on my book tonight," Matthew said. He held it up.

Richard couldn't read the name. "It looks good," he said.

"I can't read the name," Matthew said. "I can't read any of the words either. But it's about the desert. And the jungle. And rain forests. I can tell by the pictures.''

"Neat," Richard said. He started across the room. "I have to find Holly. She'll be mad if she has to wait."

He hurried out the door.

What would Ms. Rooney do when she saw that three pieces of Candy Corn were gone? he wondered.

Holly was standing at the end of the hall. "Get moving," she yelled.

Maybe Ms. Rooney wouldn't find out he had eaten them.

"I'm coming," he yelled back at Holly. "Stop rushing me."

Ms. Rooney would find out.

She always did.

Chapter 5

"Time for math buddies," Ms. Rooney said the next day.

Wayne was Richard's math buddy.

Richard went to sit with him. They were going to work on o'clocks and half pasts.

"I have three Candy Corn guesses," Wayne said.

"Lucky," Richard said.

He looked out the window. It was raining today. Lunch would be inside.

"I hope I win," Wayne said.

Richard looked at Wayne's book. It had lots of words.

Richard didn't want to tell Wayne that his book was skinnier. Almost a baby book.

Wayne was a good reader. He might win.

Timothy would probably win though.

Richard shut his eyes. If only he could win.

He'd take off the top of the jar. Put a few pieces of Candy Corn in his mouth.

"Too bad," Ms. Rooney would say. "We were going to count together. It would have been a good math lesson."

"Oh," Richard would say. "I don't know how many I just ate."

"Don't worry," Ms. Rooney would say. "You're the winner. You can eat every one of them."

"Study hard," Ms. Rooney said. "I'm going to ask some o'clocks very soon."

Wayne held up his cardboard clock. He moved the hands around. "What's that?"

"Easy," Richard said. "Two o'clock."

Wayne looked down at the card. "Are you sure?"

"Yes," said Richard.

"I'm not so good at o'clocks," Wayne said.

"Let me ask," Richard said. He took the clock. He pushed the little hand to the three. "Do you know what that is?"

Wayne stared at it. "I don't know," he said. He leaned closer. "About your sleep-over . . ."

Richard felt a little worried feeling. "I forgot," he said. "You wanted to tell me something."

"Ask," Wayne said. "I want to ask you something. Where are we going to sleep?" Wayne asked.

"In the den," Richard said. "We'll put our sleeping bags on the floor."

Wayne looked at the clock again. "I think it's three o'clock."

"Yes," Richard said. He moved the big hand to the six.

"Too hard," Wayne said.

"I think so too," Richard said.

"Who's going to sleep near Matthew?"

Richard raised his shoulders up in the air.

"I hope it's not me," Wayne said.

Richard turned the hands around the clock.

"I'm not coming if—" Wayne began.

"All right," Richard said. "You don't have to sleep near him."

"That's good," Wayne said. "If you sleep near Matthew, you'll have to wear your raincoat."

Richard started to laugh. He could see everyone asleep in his den. Everyone was wearing a yellow raincoat. Even Matthew.

Wayne poked him. "Matthew's reading a book about rain forests," he said.

"I know," said Richard.

"Rain forests," Wayne said. He started to laugh. "Matthew lives in his own rain forest."

"Is everybody ready?" Ms. Rooney asked.

Everybody went back to his own seat.

Richard took out a piece of paper. He put his heading on top.

Richard Best   **Nov. 18**
Poke St. School

He drew a bunch of circles underneath.

He was a good artist. His circles were nice and round.

Matthew's were terrible. They looked like boxes.

Matthew turned around. He looked at Richard's paper. "Nice circles," he said. Then he pointed. "I don't think you spelled *Polk* right."

Richard knelt up on his seat. He looked out the window. He tried to see the street sign outside.

But it was too far for him to see.

He erased *Poke* and thought a little.

Then he wrote *Poak*.

"Draw three o'clock," Ms. Rooney said.

In front of him Matthew counted. "Twelve. One. Two. Three."

Richard drew the hands too.

"Now draw ten o'clock," said Ms. Rooney.

"Twelve. One. Two . . ." Matthew began.

Richard thought of Matthew in a yellow raincoat.

He thought about Matthew in a rain forest.

He started to laugh again.

He hid his head behind Matthew. He didn't want Ms. Rooney to see him.

Who was going to sleep near Matthew?

He pulled his list out of his desk. It was all crumpled.

He smoothed it out. He was going to sleep next to Timothy and Alex.

Wayne would sleep on the other side of Alex.

Then what?

Noah.

Matthew could sleep near the wall.

Noah could sleep near Matthew.

He hoped Noah wouldn't find out until the last minute.

Richard sighed. He was sick of fixing up this whole thing.

"Four thirty," said Ms. Rooney.

"Shoot," said Matthew.

Richard drew a hand on the four. Then he looked out the window.

Four thirty was just too hard.

Chapter 6

It was a rainy-day lunch. Mrs. Kettle, the sixth-grade teacher, was in charge. She was the strictest teacher in the whole school.

She clapped her hands. "Are you finished eating?"

Everyone yelled yes.

"Clean your places," Mrs. Kettle said. "Go straight to the gym."

Richard didn't go straight to the gym.

He was going to sneak upstairs to his classroom. He was going to change the number on the Candy Corn jar.

If Ms. Rooney had written 103, he would write 100. If she had written 421, he would write 416. No. He would write 417. No.

He hoped she hadn't written 421.

Right after he changed the number, he was going to forget what it was.

He didn't want to cheat.

He stopped for a long drink of water at the water fountain.

He hoped Ms. Rooney wasn't in the classroom. Maybe he should wait a few minutes. Maybe he should sneak to the classroom right before the bell rang. Ms. Rooney would be downstairs in the gym with the class.

He went past the auditorium. The fifth-grade band was playing.

He opened the door a little bit.

Pom. Pom. Pom.

The drummer was banging as hard as he could. Richard could feel the pounding in his head.

He opened the door a little wider. He pounded a make-believe drum on it.

Then he spotted his sister, Holly. Her lips were squeezed over her fife.

Nobody could hear her though.

All you could hear was *pom, pom, pom.*

She frowned at him.

She shook one finger over the fife. She stopped

35

squeezing her mouth together. She opened her mouth wide. She whispered something.

Richard leaned forward.

"Get lost," she mouthed again.

Richard closed the door of the auditorium.

Someone tapped him on the shoulder.

It was Timothy Barbiero. He had a book in his hand. A big fat book.

"Hi, Richard," Timothy said. "Getting ready for your Thanksgiving sleep-over?"

Richard nodded.

Noah Greene came from around the corner. "Hey, you guys," he said.

"What about Matthew?" Timothy asked. "Is he coming to your party?"

"Yeah," Noah said. "I was going to ask you that too."

Richard looked back toward the auditorium.

The band had stopped playing. Everything was still.

"Matthew?" Richard said.

"Who is going to sleep near Matthew?"

"I'm not," Timothy said.

"No," Richard said. "You're sleeping near me. We're going to have a great time."

"I'm not sleeping near Matthew," Noah said.

Richard leaned forward. "It's my sleep-over. I'm the one who says where everyone is going to sleep."

"Then I'm not coming," Noah said.

Mrs. Avery, the music teacher, came out to the hall. "Aren't you supposed to be in the gym?" she asked.

"We're going right now," Richard said.

They turned and started for the stairs.

"Listen, Noah," Richard said. "You've got to come."

"I'm not—" Noah began.

"All right," Richard said. "Maybe Alex will sleep near Matthew."

"Are you crazy?" Timothy said. "Nobody is going to sleep near Matthew."

Noah started to laugh. "Nobody but the beast."

37

Richard kicked at the stairs. "Not me. I'm going to tell him to sleep behind the TV set."

"Good idea," Noah said.

"Nobody will get wet that way," Timothy said.

Richard followed them into the gym. How was he going to tell Matthew he had to sleep behind the TV?

The bell rang. Suddenly he remembered the Candy Corn jar.

It was too late to change the number. He'd do it tomorrow.

He hoped nobody would win before then.

Chapter 7

It was guessing time.

Emily Arrow had four guesses.

Dawn Bosco and Wayne had seven.

Timothy Barbiero had twenty-one.

"How many guesses do you have?" Matthew asked Richard.

Richard felt his new tooth. It was getting bigger.

Matthew turned and poked him. "I said—"

"One," Richard said. "One guess."

"Luckier than me," Matthew said. "I don't even have one."

Richard looked at Matthew. Suddenly he wanted to hit Matthew right on his fat nose.

Matthew was spoiling his whole Thanksgiving sleep-over party.

Emily Arrow leaned over the jar. "Nine hundred one," she said.

Ms. Rooney shook her head.

"Nine forty-two."

Ms. Rooney shook her head.

Emily stared at the jar. She counted a little bit. "Six hundred sixty-eleven."

Ms. Rooney smiled. "No such number, Emily."

Richard held his breath.

Emily looked down at her red sneakers. "Three hundred," she said slowly, "forty-eight . . . no, nine. Three hundred forty-nine."

"Sorry, Emily," said Ms. Rooney.

Richard crossed his fingers. Suppose someone won before he changed the number?

Matthew poked him again. "I hope you win, Beast," he said. "I have all my fingers crossed. And all my toes."

"Me too," Richard said.

Timothy Barbiero was getting ready to guess.

He looked as if he were thinking very hard.

Too hard, Richard thought. Twenty-one guesses were a lot.

Timothy started his guesses.

Everyone in the class looked worried.

But Timothy was wrong.

Matthew smiled at Richard.

At last it was Richard's turn. "Richard Best," said Ms. Rooney. "One guess."

"One guess," Dawn Bosco said. "That's all."

Timothy Barbiero started to laugh a little.

"You need only one guess to win," Matthew said.

"That's right," said Ms. Rooney.

Richard swallowed hard. Should he say seven hundred? Should he say nine hundred?

He took a deep breath. "Four hundred," he said. He watched Ms. Rooney's face.

She started to shake her head.

"And sixty," Richard added.

"I'm sorry," Ms. Rooney said.

"Sixty-two," Richard said.

Ms. Rooney tapped the top of the jar. "I'll give you a hint. Everyone is guessing too many."

Richard sighed. He should have guessed three hundred.

Everyone opened his book. Everyone wanted to read as fast as he could.

Richard wanted to read too. But he couldn't stop thinking about his sleep-over.

He took out a piece of drawing paper. He drew a circle for a head. He made a long balloon body. Then he put stick-out ears on the circle.

It looked like Matthew.

It made Richard angry to look at it.

Matthew was spoiling the whole sleep-over.

Richard was sick of sitting in back of Matthew.

He was sick of smelling him all day long.

He took a black crayon out of his desk. Then he drew a big *X* over the boy in his drawing.

He'd like to draw a big *X* over Matthew.

Chapter 8

"Hold up your apples," Ms. Rooney said the next day.

Richard looked around. Emily Arrow had a big red apple in her hand. Wayne had a yellow one.

Everyone was going to make applesauce.

Everyone but Richard.

He slid down in his seat.

"I don't see your apple," Ms. Rooney said.

"I left it home," he said.

Matthew turned around. He was holding a greenish apple. "You can have half of mine," he said.

Richard made a face. He didn't want to share Matthew's apple. Matthew's wet-the-bed apple.

Richard reached into his pocket. He pulled out a rubber band. He wound it around his finger until the tip of his pinkie turned purplish red.

Then he remembered someone had said you

could get blood poisoning that way. Maybe you could die.

He took the rubber band off.

"Hey," Matthew said. "Do you want to share?"

"No, thanks," he told Matthew. "I don't want your green apple."

Matthew turned to the front of the room again.

Richard could see that one of Matthew's ears stuck out farther than the other.

Right now both of Matthew's ears looked red.

Dawn Bosco raised her hand. "My mother gave me a box of raisins too," she said. "For the applesauce."

"That's nice," Ms. Rooney said.

"That's terrible," Richard said. He felt a mean feeling inside.

Ms. Rooney put a big pot on her desk. "I have some nice cold water in the pot," she said. "We'll put the apples in . . ."

"And the raisins," Dawn said.

"Yes," said Ms. Rooney. "And then we'll go

45

down to the cafeteria. We'll put our applesauce on the stove to cook."

Everyone rushed up to Ms. Rooney's desk.

Richard went up to the front too. He leaned against the chalkboard.

"Now," said Ms. Rooney. "I'll cut up the apples."

Ms. Rooney kept cutting and cutting.

Richard sighed. He leaned on one foot and then on the other. It took a long time to make applesauce.

Dawn Bosco kept saying, "Can I put the raisins in now? Can I?"

"I hate raisins," Richard said, even though he loved them.

At last Ms. Rooney cut the last apple.

Dawn dumped in the raisins.

Then the class lined up. They went downstairs to the cafeteria.

Richard looked around. There were a skillion pieces of bread on the counter. The cafeteria lady was putting a little dab of butter on each one of them.

47

She wiped her hands on her apron. She put the applesauce pot on the stove.

"Let us know when it's ready," Ms. Rooney said.

The class marched back to the room.

"Reading time," said Ms. Rooney.

"Shoot," said Matthew.

Richard and Emily and Alex and Matthew had to go to Room 100. They were extra-help readers.

"Don't worry," said Ms. Rooney. "Even if the applesauce is ready, we won't eat till you get back."

"Who cares?" Richard said.

"What's the matter with you today?" Matthew asked.

Richard didn't answer him. He ran his fingers over the bricks in the wall.

Mrs. Paris was waiting. "I heard your class was making applesauce," she said. "Lucky."

"Unlucky," Richard said. "It's probably full of germs."

"Do you think so?" Emily asked.

48

"No," said Mrs. Paris. "When it cooks—"

"Matthew's germs," Richard said.

"When it cooks," Mrs. Paris said, "the germs are boiled away." She frowned at Richard.

Richard looked down at his almost baby reading book. "Not Matthew's," he said.

"That's not nice," Alex said.

"You're not so nice either," Richard said. "I bet you don't want to sleep near Matthew at my sleep-over."

"Let's open our books," said Mrs. Paris.

"I'm reading a lot," Emily said. "I'm trying to win the Candy Corn contest."

Richard snorted. "You'll never win."

Mrs. Paris put her book down. "What's the matter with everyone today?" she asked.

Richard took a quick look at Matthew. Matthew looked as if he were going to cry.

"It's good to tell the truth . . ." Mrs. Paris began.

"That's what I say," Alex said.

"But . . ." Mrs. Paris pushed her eyeglasses

up on her nose. "It is not helpful to talk about people's problems." She looked around the table. "At least not in front of everyone."

"That's right," said Emily.

"When do you think you might talk about someone's problems?" Mrs. Paris asked.

"Never," said Emily.

"Never," Matthew mumbled.

"Well," said Richard. "Maybe . . ."

Mrs. Paris stared at him. "Maybe what?"

"Maybe if you could help?"

"Yes," said Mrs. Paris.

"I don't need any help," said Emily.

"Let's think of a problem," said Mrs. Paris.

"All right," said Alex.

"I know one," Richard said quickly. "I forgot my apple."

"That's a good problem," Emily said.

Richard looked down at the table. Suddenly he remembered that Matthew had tried to help.

"That was a problem," Mrs. Paris said. "How could someone help Richard?"

"Share," said Emily.

"True," said Mrs. Paris.

"Not tell him he was terrible," said Emily.

"True," said Mrs. Paris again. She looked around at everyone. "When someone has a problem," she said, "help if you can. But not in front of other people."

"And shut your mouth if you can't," said Emily.

"Exactly," said Mrs. Paris.

Just then the door opened. It was Emily's friend Jill Simon.

"Ms. Rooney said the applesauce is ready," Jill said.

Mrs. Paris stood up. "Warm applesauce. Wonderful." She looked around at the table. "All right, everyone. You may go back."

Richard stood up. He didn't feel the mean feeling anymore. It was gone.

He felt worse now. He had a terrible feeling inside. He knew Matthew was still crying a little.

He wanted to cry too. He wanted to tell Matthew he was sorry.

He turned around to tell Matthew.

But Mrs. Paris was talking. "Will you erase the blackboard for me, Matthew?" she asked. "It will only take a minute."

"Sure," Matthew said.

Everyone else went back to the classroom.

Ms. Rooney gave out the applesauce.

But Richard had a lump in his throat. He knew he'd never be able to swallow. "No, thank you," he told Ms. Rooney.

Matthew came in a minute later. He told Ms. Rooney no, thank you too.

Richard tore up his *X* picture of Matthew. He was sorry he had ever drawn it.

Chapter 9

The next morning the bell rang three times. Then it rang three times again.

Fire drill!

Richard loved fire drills.

"Get your coats quickly," Ms. Rooney said.

Richard grabbed his sweater. He lined up behind Matthew.

"Hey, Matthew," he whispered.

"No talking," Ms. Rooney said. "Remember, this is a fire drill."

The class followed Ms. Rooney out into the hall.

All the other classes were spilling out into the hall too.

Richard saw his sister, Holly. She was marching along in front of her best friend, Joanne.

Richard waved at them.

Holly made a face.

She was still mad at him because of last night.

He had drawn some clocks on the back of her homework.

By accident.

He thought it was scrap paper.

Outside it was cold. Richard put his face up to the sun to get warm. Then he watched a four-year-old across the street. She was waving a big red leaf at them.

He poked Matthew.

Matthew looked at the little girl and grinned. Then he faced front again.

Richard looked at Matthew's ears. He leaned a little closer to him.

Matthew didn't smell as much today. Maybe it was because of the cold air.

"Listen, Matthew," he whispered. "I'm sorry about yesterday."

Mrs. Kettle snapped her fingers at him from half a block away. "Be quiet, young man," she called. "This is a fire drill."

Everyone looked at Richard.

Ms. Rooney frowned.

But Matthew didn't turn around.

Maybe Matthew hadn't heard him.

As soon as they went back to the classroom, he'd tell Matthew he was sorry.

He thought about telling Holly he was sorry too.

No. It was a fire drill.

She'd have to wait until tonight.

The bell rang. Everyone marched inside again.

Richard made a beast face when he passed Holly in the hall.

"Brat," she whispered.

Back in the classroom Ms. Rooney told everyone to take out notebooks.

It was time to copy boardwork.

The boardwork was a story about Thanksgiving and Pilgrims and Indians.

Richard picked up his pencil. *The first Thanksgiving was held in Plymouth,* he wrote.

Matthew turned around. "I can't come to your Thanksgiving sleep-over."

"I'm sorry," Richard said at the same time. "I didn't mean to say—"

"I can't come to—" Matthew began again.

He looked at Matthew's face. Matthew looked funny. No, Matthew looked sad.

"Why can't you come?" Richard said.

Matthew turned to the front. He looked back over his shoulder. "Because."

Richard picked up his pencil. He tapped Matthew. "Did your mother say you can't come?"

Matthew didn't say anything.

Richard copied the next sentence. *The Pilgrims invited everyone.*

He waited a minute. "Matthew? Is it because I said those mean things?"

Matthew shook his head. "I'm going on vacation."

"Oh," Richard said. He felt better. Much better. He gave Matthew a little punch. "Where are you going?"

"Plymouth," Matthew said.

"Where the Pilgrims landed?"

57

Matthew nodded.

"Lucky," Richard said. "Boy, are you lucky!"

"Yeah," Matthew said.

Richard wrote the rest of the story. He was glad Matthew was going to an exciting place.

He was glad he didn't have to worry about Matthew coming to his sleep-over anymore.

He dusted off his paper. He saw that he had written *Plymouth* twice.

He didn't know anyone who had ever gone to Plymouth. He didn't even know where it was.

He leaned forward. "Matthew? Where's Plymouth?"

Matthew rolled his pencil on the floor. He bent over to pick it up. "Florida," he said. "In the middle of Florida."

"Oh," Richard said. He stood up. It was time for a drink.

He went to the front of the room. He looked back at Matthew.

Matthew wasn't writing his boardwork. He was just sitting there.

Maybe he was thinking about going to Plymouth.

Richard closed the classroom door behind him. He walked to the water fountain.

He wondered why Matthew didn't look happy.

He'd be happy if he were going to Plymouth. It was almost as good as going to a sleep-over.

Chapter 10

Today was assembly day. The fifth grade was putting on a play: *The Pilgrims Come to America*.

Richard knew all about it. His sister, Holly, was a Pilgrim mother. She was going to wear a long gray bathrobe and a white cardboard hat.

At home she said her part about a hundred times a day.

But today he wouldn't hear Holly in the assembly.

As soon as everyone said the Pledge he was going to sneak out.

He was going straight upstairs. He was going to change the number on the Candy Corn jar.

It was his last chance. Tomorrow was the last day of school before Thanksgiving.

Mr. Mancina turned off the lights. Next to him Emily was trying to read in the dark.

Richard kept his head down. He sneaked out of his seat.

Mrs. Kettle was standing at the back. "Where are you going, young man?" she asked.

Richard jumped. "I have to go to the—"

"The play just started," she said. She opened the door for him. "Why didn't you go to the bathroom before you came in here?"

Richard put his head down a little more.

"Hurry up," she said.

He raced down the hall. He turned the corner. Then he headed upstairs.

No one was in Room 113.

He closed the door. He tiptoed to Ms. Rooney's desk.

He picked up the jar carefully. He'd hate to drop it.

He might as well drop himself.

He laughed a little at the thought of dropping himself.

He turned the jar on its side. He looked underneath.

Matthew was right. There was a big number on the bottom.

278.

He tried not to think about 278.

He'd have to forget that number in a few minutes.

He took his pencil out of his pocket.

No good. The number 278 was written in ink.

He put the jar on the floor. It would be safe there.

He ran back to his desk. He pulled everything out. In the back was a pen.

He raced back to Ms. Rooney's desk.

He counted on his fingers. Not 278 anymore. Now it would be . . . 277 . . . 276 . . . 275.

Was that right?

He counted again. Yes. He had to change the 8 to a 5.

The classroom door opened.

Richard jumped.

"What are you doing?" Matthew asked.

"I didn't cheat," Richard said. "Don't worry."

Matthew walked toward his desk. "Are you looking at the number?"

"Just a little bit," Richard said.

"Oh." Matthew reached into his desk. "I came to get some of my Fluffernutter sandwich."

"I did something terrible," Richard said.

"Worse than cheating?" Matthew asked.

"I ate three pieces of Candy Corn."

Matthew wiped some Fluffernutter off his mouth.

"I have to change the number," Richard said.

"You can't do that," Matthew said. "I think Ms. Rooney may check the fingerprints."

Richard stared at him. "Fingerprints?"

"She'll see that the number looks different. . . ."

"No," Richard said. "I'll do it so you can't tell."

"You can't write like Ms. Rooney." Matthew sat on a front desk. "Keep that jar away from me. I don't want to be a cheater."

Richard shook the jar a little. Then he moved it away from Matthew.

Matthew was shaking his head. He looked sad.

"Ms. Rooney may take the jar to the police. Your fingerprints will be all over it."

Richard stepped back. "I think you're right."

"I'm sorry," Matthew said. "I wish you could change the number."

He and Matthew went back down the stairs.

"I'm glad you came up to the classroom," Richard said. "I could have been in a lot of trouble."

Matthew nodded his head.

They opened the auditorium doors and tiptoed in.

Up on the stage Holly was saying her part. She was talking so loud, she was almost yelling.

"It was a hard year in Plymouth," she said.

Richard slid into his seat. He said the words with Holly. "It was the right thing to do. Now we have a good place to live. We have food to eat."

Richard thought about the Candy Corn jar. He was glad he hadn't changed the number. Somehow that wouldn't have been the right thing to do.

Somebody else came on the stage. It was Arthur Knight in a blue suit. "Yes," he said. "It was a hard year in Plymouth, Massachusetts. But now we will have a Thanksgiving dinner."

Richard watched the curtain close. He said Massachusetts to himself. "Mas-sa-chew-setts."

He loved the sound of it on his tongue.

The class filed out of the auditorium.

"Massa-chew," sang Richard as he marched. "Massachew-chew-chew-setts." He tried not to think about the Candy Corn jar.

He poked Matthew in the back. "Hey. Plymouth is in Massachusetts."

Matthew raised his shoulders up in the air.

"You said it was in Florida—where Dawn Bosco's grandmother lives."

Matthew didn't say anything. His face looked a little red. So did his ears.

Richard marched into Room 113. Maybe Matthew wasn't going to Plymouth. Maybe he had made the whole thing up.

He wondered why.

Suddenly he had a terrible feeling. Suddenly he knew why Matthew had lied.

Richard sat down in his seat. Matthew knew he didn't want him at the sleep-over.

In front of him Matthew was trying to read his rain forest book. He was still on page one.

Richard opened his own book.

If only he hadn't said those mean things to Matthew.

He was almost sorry he was having a sleep-over.

Chapter 11

Today was the last day of school before Thanksgiving.

Richard took a long time walking to school. He kept thinking about the Candy Corn number.

It was the last day for the contest.

He was going to be in trouble when he didn't win.

He said some numbers in his head. He tried to forget 278.

He saw Matthew going into the schoolyard. He wished he could forget about Matthew too.

Matthew must feel terrible about the party.

Richard knew he'd feel terrible too.

"290," he said in a loud voice. "280. 315. 876." He kicked at a pile of brown leaves. "278," he said in a little voice.

A real Pilgrim would tell Ms. Rooney about the Candy Corn, Richard thought. A real Pilgrim would say that he had eaten three pieces.

The bell rang in the schoolyard. Ms. Rooney's line started for the doors.

"492," Richard yelled. He ran to catch up.

Matthew saw him coming. "Hurry," he yelled.

The monitor told Richard to stop running.

He had to get in line with the third-graders.

Matthew turned around. "Good news," he called.

The monitor yelled at everyone to be quiet.

Richard wondered what Matthew's news was. Matthew looked happy.

Matthew was his friend.

Matthew should be coming to his sleep-over.

"326," Richard whispered. He wouldn't be happy if his friend didn't want him at a sleep-over. He wouldn't be smiling.

In the classroom everyone was running around.

Ms. Rooney was late today.

Matthew met him at the door. "Guess what?" he said. "I just saved your life."

Richard looked at Matthew's face. He looked at Matthew's stick-out ears.

It would be terrible if Matthew didn't come to his sleep-over party.

"Matthew," he said. "I want you to come."

Matthew held out his hand. "Look," he said.

"Please come to my sleep-over," Richard said. He looked down. Matthew had three fat pieces of Candy Corn in his hand.

Richard looked at the Candy Corn. He wondered if it had the wet-the-bed smell.

But today Matthew smelled different.

Not a lot different. Just a little different.

"Put them in the jar," Matthew said.

Richard opened his eyes wide. "You just saved my life, Matthew," he said.

Ms. Rooney came rushing in the door. "Whew," she said. "I had a flat tire. I'm sorry I'm late."

Richard followed her to the desk.

She looked up. "Yes, Richard?"

"I ate three pieces of Candy Corn. Matthew gave me three more. He didn't want me to get in trouble. I thought I'd better tell you though."

Ms. Rooney opened her mouth into a fat O.

Matthew opened the top of the jar. He dropped in the Candy Corn.

"A Pilgrim wouldn't have eaten three pieces of Candy Corn," Ms. Rooney said. Then she smiled. "But you're a true Pilgrim for telling me."

Then Ms. Rooney clapped her hands. "Please stop running around," she told the class.

Everyone went to his seat.

Richard put his books away. "I forgot to say thank you," he whispered to Matthew.

"It's all right," Matthew said.

"You've got to come to my sleep-over," Richard said.

Matthew looked out the window. "I guess I could come," he said.

"Right," said Richard. He thought about Mrs. Paris. He remembered what she had said. *When someone has a problem, help if you can.* "Maybe," he told Matthew, "you could take a bath."

"For a party I would," Matthew said. "In fact, I've been trying to take a bath more than usual."

"That's good," Richard said.

"Yeah," Matthew said. "I never liked baths much, but Mrs. Paris gave me some bubble bath."

"Lucky," Richard said.

Matthew nodded. "She gave it to me when I erased the board for her." He took out his library book. "I'm up to the last sentence on page one."

Richard listened as Matthew read.

"M-mmm-ost," Matthew sounded out. "Most of the ttt-ime ccc-croc-o-croc-odiles live in rain forests."

Matthew slammed the book shut. "One page," he said to Richard. "One guess."

"Good," Richard said.

"That reminds me," Matthew said. "I'm bringing an alarm clock to your sleep-over."

"Really?" Richard said.

"I'll get up a couple of times," Matthew said. "To go to the bathroom."

"Oh," Richard said. "That's a great idea."

"It was my mother's idea," Matthew said.

"All right, class," said Ms. Rooney. "Who has guesses?"

Timothy raised his hand. "I have five."

"I have three," yelled Emily.

"Me too," said Jill Simon.

"114," said Richard under his breath. "412." He raised his hand. "I have a guess."

"Me too," Matthew said. "I have a guess. A big one."

278, Richard said in his head.

Everyone went up to Ms. Rooney's desk. Jill guessed first.

Timothy took two guesses. Then he stopped. "I'm going to think for a few minutes," he said.

Then it was Richard's guess. He wondered what a Pilgrim would do.

"I think," he began. He looked at Ms. Rooney. "200 and . . ." he said slowly. "200 and 70 . . ."

Ms. Rooney leaned forward a little. She was smiling.

"No," said Richard. "300. I mean, 342."

Ms. Rooney sat back. She shook her head. "Timothy?"

"I think it's in the 200's," he said. "How about 241?"

Ms. Rooney shook her head.

"290?"

"How about Matthew?" Ms. Rooney asked.

Matthew squeezed his eyes together. "299," he said. Then he opened his eyes.

"My turn," Emily Arrow said. She took a deep breath. She looked at the jar. "I think . . ." she said, and stopped. "I think it's . . . 278."

"That's it," Ms. Rooney yelled.

Emily jumped up and down in her red sneakers. "I don't believe it," she yelled.

"I don't believe it either," Timothy said.

"Now we'll count them," Ms. Rooney said.

Richard smiled at Matthew.

"Can we divide them up?" Emily asked. "So everyone can share?"

"You're a true Pilgrim," Ms. Rooney said. She started to count.

When they were finished counting, Ms. Rooney

75

did a big dividing example on the blackboard. "Everyone gets twenty pieces," she said.

Emily put twenty pieces on everyone's desk.

There were eighteen pieces left.

Emily gave ten to Ms. Rooney. "Mrs. Paris gets the rest," she said.

Richard put two Candy Corn pieces in his mouth. He crunched down on them. He closed his eyes to taste the sugar better.

Delicious.

He opened his eyes and gave Matthew a little tap. "Happy Thanksgiving," he said.